OH, NUTS!

Tammi Sauer   illustrated by Dan Krall

BLOOMSBURY

NEW YORK LONDON NEW DELHI SYDNEY

Text copyright © 2012 by Tammi Sauer
Illustrations copyright © 2012 by Dan Krall
All rights reserved. No part of this book may be reproduced or transmitted in any form or
by any means, electronic or mechanical, including photocopying, recording, or by any information
storage and retrieval system, without permission in writing from the publisher.

First published in the United States of America in September 2012
by Bloomsbury Books for Young Readers
www.bloomsburykids.com

For information about permission to reproduce selections from this book, write to
Permissions, Bloomsbury BFYR, 175 Fifth Avenue, New York, New York 10010

Library of Congress Cataloging-in-Publication Data
Sauer, Tammi.
Oh, nuts! / by Tammi Sauer ; illustrations by Dan Krall. — 1st U.S. ed.
p.   cm.
Summary: Chipmunks Cutesy, Blinky, and Bob want the same kind of attention people pay to other animals who live in the zoo,
but when one of their plans succeeds, they see that being noticed is not always a good thing.
ISBN 978-1-59990-466-5 (hardcover) • ISBN 978-1-59990-467-2 (reinforced)
[1. Chipmunks—Fiction. 2. Zoos—Fiction. 3. Popularity—Fiction.] I. Krall, Dan, ill. II. Title.
PZ7.S25020h 2012   [E]—dc23   2011042338

Art created digitally in Photoshop
Typeset in TypographyofCoop Forged
Book design by Regina Roff

Printed in China by Hung Hing Printing (China) Co, Ltd, Shenzhen, Guangdong
1 3 5 7 9 10 8 6 4 2 (hardcover)
1 3 5 7 9 10 8 6 4 2 (reinforced)

All papers used by Bloomsbury Publishing, Inc, are natural, recyclable products
made from wood grown in well-managed forests. The manufacturing processes
conform to the environmental regulations of the country of origin.

For my nutty family
—T. S.

For my big nut, Rachel, and my little acorn, Mia
—D. K.

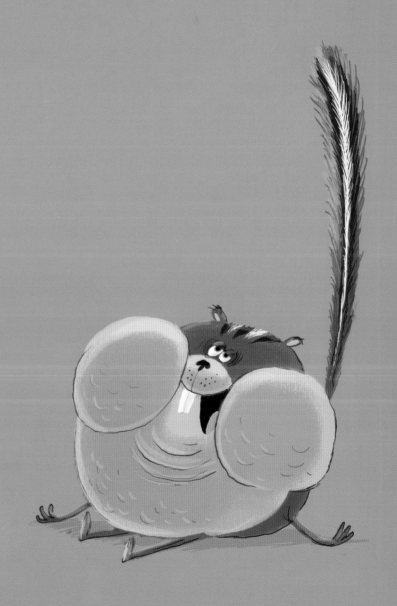

Cutesy, Blinky, and Bob lived at the zoo.

They **whooshed** through grass,

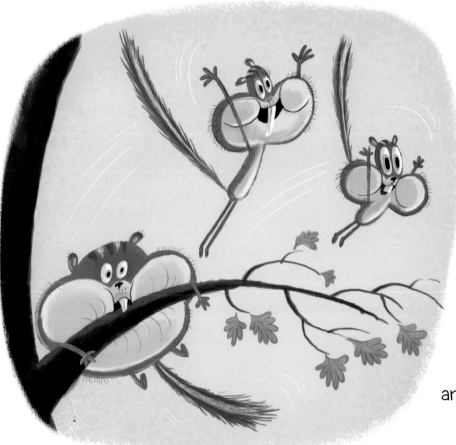

darted up trees,

and **zipped** over branches. But . . .

nobody

paid any attention to them.

Day after day, it was the same old thing.

"Ooh! Look at the tiger!"

"Wow! Watch the elephant!"

"Cool! Check out the koala!"

Blah. Blah. Blah. The chipmunks tried to ignore it.

But when the **sloth** got groupies?
"Oh, nuts."

They needed a plan.

Cutesy thought as she fluffed her fur.

Blinky thought as he tapped his foot.

And Bob? He pretty much just sat there.

"Ooh! Ooh! I know," said Cutesy. "Let's give ourselves makeovers!"

The chipmunks raided the Lost and Found, added just the right accessories,

then struck a pose.
But . . .

...everyone was too busy watching the **zebras** chew grass to notice.

Cutesy thought harder as she filed her nails.

Blinky thought even harder as he drummed an acorn.

And Bob? He pretty much just sat there.

At last, Blinky grinned. "Like, WOW, dudes. Music is the answer."

The chipmunks **spiked** their fur,
grabbed some **gear,**

then **rocked** the park.
But …

...everyone was **too busy** watching the **giraffes** flick bugs to notice.

THWACK

Cutesy thought extra hard as she **twirled** her whiskers.

Blinky thought extra, extra hard as he **strummed** a guitar.

And **Bob?** **Well.** You know.

"**Chipmunks**," said Cutesy. "It's time to play hardball."

They outran the **cheetah**.

Outstared the **owl**.

Outswam the **piranhas**.

And, for good measure, outzapped the **poison dart frog**.
But . . .

. . . everyone was too BUSY watching the POSSUM play dead to notice.

Then a **miracle** happened.

The **chipmunks scrambled** between the bars,
took their **places,**

... zoo style.

Cutesy chewed grass.

Blinky flicked bugs.

And **Bob** pretty much just played dead.

They were **great!**
They were **awesome!**
They were . . .

Cutesy, Blinky, and Bob

lived at the zoo.

Nobody paid any attention to them.

And that was just fine.

The **pigeons,** however, had plans of their own.